D1073940

NILES DISTRICT LIBRARY
NILES, MICHIGAN 49120

MAR 0 5 2003

First published in English copyright © 2001 Abbeville Press.
First published in French copyright © 1998 Editions Nathan, Paris (France). Translated by
Molly Stevens. All rights reserved under international copyright conventions. No part of
this book may be reproduced or utilized in any form or by any means, electronic or
mechanical, without permission in writing from the publisher. Inquiries should be
addressed to Abbeville Publishing Group, 22 Cortlandt Street, New York, NY 10007.
The text of this book was set in Journal Text. Printed and bound in France.

First edition
2 4 6 8 10 9 7 5 3 1

Library of Congress Card Number: 00-107675

Tom Thumb

A Fairy Tale by Charles Perrault
Illustrated by Charlotte Roederer

· Abbeville Kids ·
A Division of Abbeville Publishing Group
New York · London · Paris

JE
PER

Once upon a time, there was a poor couple—
a lumberjack and his wife—who had seven sons. Even
though they worked hard, they had very little money
and their children were always hungry.

The lumberjack and his wife worried about all of
their children, but they worried most about the youn-
gest. He was so much smaller than his brothers. In
fact, when he was born, he was no bigger than his
father's thumb, and so they called him Tom Thumb.

One night, when the parents thought the boys were in bed, the lumberjack said to his wife, "There has been practically nothing to eat for weeks now. Perhaps if we leave the boys in the forest, they will find nuts and berries and be able to survive on their own."

The wife was afraid for the children, and she would not let them go. But she knew there was no food at home, so finally she agreed.

But Tom Thumb had been hiding under his father's chair. He had heard everything!

Early the next morning, Tom Thumb gathered white pebbles from a nearby stream and put them in his pockets. Then the parents took the boys deep into the dark forest. Tom Thumb dropped the white

pebbles all along the way.

Finally, the lumberjack started cutting up some fallen trees. He told the boys to pick up the pieces of wood and put them in a pile. While they were busy, he and his wife sneaked away.

When Tom Thumb's brothers realized that their parents had left them, they began to cry. "Don't worry," said Tom Thumb. "I can find the way." And he led them home by following the pebbles.

The parents were overjoyed to see that their children were unharmed. They had been so worried about them! Later that very day, a wealthy family visited the town and bought a load of firewood from the lumberjack. The family now had money to buy food for several meals.

Soon, however, all they had left was a half loaf of stale bread. That night after the boys had gone to bed, the parents finally decided to leave their sons in the forest again. Tom Thumb was awake and he heard every word.

Early the next morning, Tom Thumb got up to gather pebbles. But when he tried to open the door, it was locked!

As he was thinking about his problem, his mother handed him a piece of bread. "I know," thought Tom Thumb, "I'll drop bread crumbs on the path!"

The parents led the boys to the darkest corner
of the forest and told them to look for mushrooms.
While they were busy, the parents quietly left.

Tom Thumb was not worried. After all, the boys
could follow his trail of bread crumbs back to their
house. But when they looked for them, the crumbs
had disappeared. The birds had eaten every one.

The boys began to walk anyway, but the longer
they walked, the more lost they became. Finally, it
got dark.

"I'll climb a tree and have a look around," said
Tom Thumb. When he reached the top of a tree, he
saw lights shining in a window not so far away. "I
see a house!" cried Tom Thumb.

"Let's go!" cheered his brothers.

Soon they were knocking at the front door of the house they had seen. A woman wearing a crown answered the door.

"Hello ma'am," said Tom Thumb. "We're lost in the forest. Could you take us in?"

"Oh, you poor children! You don't know whose house this is! My husband is an ogre who captured me, and he eats little children who come by. He'll be home any minute. You'd better come in and I'll

hide you until he goes out again tomorrow."

As soon as they were inside, they heard the ogre coming. "Hurry! Hide under this bed!" said the princess. The last boy was crawling under the bed when the ogre came in.

"I smell fresh meat!" the ogre said, sniffing left and right. Then he went straight to the bed and pulled out the seven brothers one by one. He was pointing a big knife at one of the boys when his wife said, "It's so late. They'll keep 'til morning. Sit down and have your dinner."

"Humph. I guess you're right," said the ogre. He

was very hungry and food was already on the table.

As the wife led the boys to another bed in the room, Tom Thumb looked back at the bed they had crawled under. In it were the ogre's seven daughters, sound asleep. On each of their heads was a gold crown. This gave Tom Thumb an idea.

After the ogre and his wife had gone to bed, Tom Thumb got up. He put the boys' hats on the ogre's daughters, and their crowns on the boys.

His plan worked. The ogre woke up at midnight to check on his breakfast—the boys. He walked over to the bed where the boys were sleeping, but when he put

out his hand and felt the crowns, he stopped.

"I almost made a horrible mistake!" he thought. So he went over to his daughters' bed and felt the hats on their heads. "Ah, here they are," he thought. "I don't want them to escape." Then, in one quick movement, the ogre gathered up his sleeping daughters in their blanket and tied the corners together to make one big bundle. "Now they'll keep 'til morning," he said.

NILES DISTRICT LIBRARY
NILES, MICHIGAN 49120

Tom Thumb had been awake the whole time. As soon as he heard the ogre snoring again, he woke up his brothers. Without a sound they took some of the ogre's food and sneaked out of the house.

In the forest they found a stream, which they followed all night. By the time the ogre woke up in the morning, the boys were almost home. They could see their parents' house.

The ogre was furious when he discovered that the boys had tricked him. "Wife!" he shouted. "Give me my seven-league boots! I'm going to catch those scoundrels."

The seven-league boots were magic. Anyone who wore them could cover many miles with just one step. When the boys saw the ogre jumping from mountain to mountain and coming toward them, they hid behind a rock. They were just in time. The ogre stopped a few feet away from them and lay down to rest. Soon he was asleep.

Tom Thumb told his brothers to hurry home with the food they had taken from the ogre's house. Then quietly, oh so quietly, he took the seven-league boots off the ogre's feet and put them on his own. And

because they were magical, the boots shrank to fit Tom Thumb's tiny feet. In just a few steps he was at the royal palace.

When the ogre woke up, he couldn't find the boys anywhere in the forest. Even worse, his magic boots were gone. So he set off on the long walk back to his home deep in the forest.

The king had seen Tom Thumb leaping easily from mountain to mountain, and so he hired the boy as a royal messenger. Every month Tom Thumb sent money to his family so that they would never be hungry again.

Finally, the day came when Tom Thumb said good-bye to the king, and returned home. His father,

mother, and six brothers gave him a hero's welcome. For even though he was small, he had accomplished great things.

Look carefully at these objects and animals.

Can you find where they appear in the story?